M000106339

This book is dedicated to my friend,
Tecumseh.
May his spirit always live
in the stone without time.

There is a glossary in the back of this book for uncommon and Sasquatch terms

Cross Over

1

As I descend the switchback, I cannot help but think of Ted Kaczynski, now a bit of a kindred spirit in a bizarre and opaque way. If that lunatic could survive and win over the Sasquatch in Cross Over, then I shouldn't have a whole hell of a lot to worry about.

Yet, I am self-conscious knowing I must look as crazy as he was, belting out "Hi-Ho, Hi-Ho, off to work I go," at the top of my lungs in this foreign universe of Sasquatch I know very little about.

Now that my ruckus has gotten their attention, I notice that I have caused the crew of Sasquatch to abandon control of their raft. It is drifting sideways because one of them has dropped their tow line. Another Sasquatch has at least temporarily forgotten his duties in order to gesticulate wildly at the strange singing human descending down upon them.

In the resultant confusion, there is at once a frantic tug of war with the raft and its remaining crew as the raft tries to spin out of control. Then with emergency efforts by all the Sasquatch once again refocused on the task, my descent is ignored and forgotten. I might just as well be a pesky horsefly buzzing in a nether world out of reach. I'm just hoping a ticked off bruiser doesn't decide to turn and give me a good swat when I reach the beach. I don't think I'd be likely to survive.

As I set foot on the spit of sand, the raft is being stabilized with large wooden stakes already driven deep to loop the raft's ropes. With some quick overhand knots by the Sasquatch, I am suddenly once again the focus of a dozen shocked faces. For some strange reason I get the impression they are more petrified of me than I am of them.

The combined force of their powerful presence all turned toward me has halted my forward progress like a wall. Time has come to a standstill. Though I am not exactly afraid, I am frozen. How long we have been staring at each other with just a few feet of sand between us, is difficult to discern. Probably only seconds, but it feels like forever. The first thing that comes into my mind is the Stone Without Time. Its presence in the palm of my hand registers as my one and only weapon. In what seems like slow motion, I pull it from my pocket and hold up for the towering Sasquatch to see.

"Loquius," I say. "Loquius."

And yes, that is the honored password in Cross Over. Their gazes turn to each other as the name registers and subdues a major portion of their fears and confusion. There is a quick paced discussion of sorts before their attention returns to the strange little creature staring meekly up at them.

Once again, I am overwhelmed by their size. I once saw a huge grizzly stand on his hind legs to impress me with his attributes, and as big as that grizzly was, I do not believe that he'd have the courage necessary to stand up to a Sasquatch. These guys are not just big, they are Bigfoot construction worker enormous.

"Loquius," I repeat, trying to keep any hint of uncertainty from my voice.

Again, there is an animated discussion with hands and arms gesticulating about. There seems to be a faction of discord from two or three of the crew as I look on. The look in their eyes and their postures suggest I would be in Bigfoot trouble if not for the vote tally registering in my favor.

One of the Sasquatch separates from the group and in three long strides is towering over me. I can smell the damp hair, it's not unlike the smell of a wet dog after getting a bath, not repulsive, but also not a sweet odor of freshness.

"Oooo-de-de-do?" I am sure he is asking me a question. Such a strange sounding language, kind of like R2-D2 in Star Wars.

I only have one answer. "Loquius?" I ask, and just like with the Sasquatch wolf boy, I raise my hand to my brow and pretend to look.

Big boy turns back to the group and appears to get confirmation from the other's yet bewildered looks. He raises his huge arm and points at the raft, then kneels and looks me in the face. With a finger the circumference of my wrist, he draws a squiggly line in the sand. He points once more to the raft and moves his finger up the squiggly line to a point where he jabs his finger in the sand.

"Pariseema," he says. "Loquius Pariseema."

I am caught completely off guard when his big arm reaches out and encircles my waist. I am hefted into the air like a rag doll and carried to the raft where I am handed up to another Sasquatch that deposits me on a bed of fresh kenaf.

With a flurry of motion, the crew is back to work and I've acquired a one-way ticket to Pariseema.

2

The river is a vast source of navigation and activity as we traverse the first few bends. I can see Sasquatch fishing from the shore with long cane poles. Traveling in our wake are small rafts with four to six oars. I notice the tell-tale mounds of Bigfoot homes appearing along the bank where a few wolves are out pacing and barking at our passing.

The first really strange sight is that of a structure that looks similar to a Middle Eastern temple. It is white and dome-shaped, not covered with earth and plants like the homes. It looks to have borrowed its design from human geodesic engineering. Once again, I am struck by the largesse of the facade built to accommodate the Sasquatch instead of man.

We continue upstream and the temple structure finally fades and disappears as we wend a big bend where the river opens into a medium sized lake. Here, the raft's ropes are coiled, and huge oars are mounted in oar locks as the raft is muscled out into the deep. The water is a staggering deep blue in contrast to the light blue, cloud dappled sky. The air has an invigorating quality that makes me feel energized. I can feel the molecules in my lungs rejoice from the purity.

The lake is cradled by hills and dotted with many smaller geodesic structures built from the same white material that dominated the temple. They are reminiscent of hillside homes you might see above Santa Barbara, California.

At the end of the lake is a pure white city of these geodesic structures. It climbs the hillside from the shore to its pinnacle like a huge overflowing glacier. All the building's domes are white, broken only by off-white shadows, green trees and flowering bushes. It fills me with a sense of cleanliness that no human city has been able to accomplish. Maybe it is just the whiteness and the simple barrier of distance, but it emanates a beauty I have never experienced from a mass populace of human engineering.

The Sasquatch are once again chanting, and their oars are biting the water in perfect harmony. The raft is humming along and rapidly parting company with the river's shore. I am enjoying my trip. It is like a fantasy inside a dream in which I am wide awake.

3

The port of entry into white city of Pariseema is still the river, it does not end, but wends into the midst of the city itself. Here, the river's current is lazy, and the river has widened. The banks have been contained by walls of the same white material of which the whole city's structures have been built. There are Sasquatch busy everywhere along the banks in a bustling dance of commerce. It is just like in any human cityscape, except there is a lack of noisy machinery and automobiles, so the city's motion is eerily muzzled and sounds more like the hum of a beehive than the cacophony of a place like Chicago or Detroit.

The oarsmen deftly maneuver our raft into an open stall in front of the largest building in Pariseema and tie us off. A stairway splits the river wall and climbs into a bowl-shaped rotunda at the building's base. For the moment, it is empty, but I get a vision of the giant space filled with cheering Sasquatch. I can imagine Loquius standing on the large staged edifice delivering profound edicts and decrees to an eager populace. I am certain this is the house of The Council of Elders of which Leeitus has referred.

My arrival, however, is not greeted by fanfare. It is not greeted at all. Instead, I am abruptly plucked from my cozy bed of kenaf by a big muscled Sasquatch and deposited without comment onto the empty stairs leading up and across the empty rotunda.

The raft is swiftly unleashed and maneuvered away as the oarsmen resume their unified thrusts and chants.

I spontaneously wave and the tiller man along with a few idle Sasquatch wave back.

4

My climb to meet Loquius is quite cumbersome because of the radical spacing of the rotunda steps, built for the gait of a Sasquatch instead of a man with smaller strides like myself. Strangely, it harkens back to childhood where everything seemed too large in scale for my little body to easily navigate and comprehend.

The white material of the stairs and rotunda reminds me of plaster. It is hard and dense, with embedded strands of fiber and white pebbles. It is miraculously crack free except for the engineered stress joints that appear every few feet. There are few blemishes and not a speck of trash other than natural debris like leaves and bird droppings. It is all quite impressive.

As I near the top of the stairs I am abuzz with a curious and awed excitement about what may be in store for a wayward human when he knocks on the huge wooden doors at the top.

The view from the rotunda pinnacle is breathtaking. The forests roll away on a lush carpet of greens, tinged by golds and bright oranges where autumn has already touched Cross Over with an icy finger. I can smell the season's fresh harvests in the air.

As I turn away from contemplating the scene, the doors begin swinging inward and I am greeted by two columns of Sasquatch standing at attention in an ornately living foyer. The walls are covered in climbing roses and other flowering vines of which I am not familiar. The ceiling is an intricate lattice of ropes, also covered in vines and fragrant blooms. The aroma is as intoxicating as the robust and vibrant visuals. In the entrance's center is a fountain and pond gathered by a slightly conical floor.

As I proceed into the chamber, the column of Sasquatch fall into formation behind me — two abreast. The only sounds are my footsteps on the stone floor and a slight rustle from the movement of the Sasquatch behind me. There's almost a sense of deja vu as I continue to walk toward an arched opening framed by two more hand-hewn wooden doors.

The doors open quietly and Loquius is standing there in greeting. Behind him are several more Sasquatch that look very old. Their hair is white-silver and their faces deeply etched by the culmination of thousands of years.

"Welcome," Loquius gestures with open arms.

"Once again, you have proven worthy of being the chosen one. There is great interest as well as skepticism behind your appearance in Pariseema before the Council of Elders. These are trying times for this world and yours."

As on another occasion, I am compelled to extend my index finger and the gesture is simultaneously reciprocated with a gentle and prolonged touch by the huge index finger of Loquius. I see nods and soft smiles from the elders directly in my view.

"I took heed in your advice," I say. "I followed the Stone Without Time. I saw you there beckoning me, and here I am."

Again, there are nods from the elders.

"I believe that in your world you have a noise box called a television, and another called a computer. We have seen these things by peeking through your windows. In those noise boxes are many voices and pictures quite different from those you see and hear in the Stone Without Time. In your world, those electronic voices and pictures look to be determined to overwhelm and entice a desired agreement and predetermined outcome from the listener. In the Stone Without Time, the voices and pictures you hear and see are thought created, they are reflections of your own mind and heart. You are here because of your own self-determined purposes that have found agreement within our Sasquatch universe."

I smile. It is like a huge weight being lifted from my shoulders because I know what he has said is the truth. I weened myself away from TV years ago, and my use of the computer is limited to mostly those things that serve and enhance my abilities to be happily productive. My life has dramatically changed for the better since I am no longer bombarded with the voices and pictures of big money and media puppeteers.

"I understand," I acknowledge. "I am not hypnotized nor subliminally directed like many of my fellow humans. No one thinks for me, I think for myself. I have come to be here on my own volition."

"Yes, your visions are your own. That is the only way the Stone Without Time can work. It has no value to those that are not pure of thought nor heart. That is why you were chosen."

I am directed into an intimate chamber and a seat near the center of a serpentine table made from a single tree. I count thirteen elders as they file in and gather with their gnarled fingers placed on the backs of their chairs. They remain standing until a nod from Loquius puts them in their seats.

Then all eyes are leveled on me and I am blasted by thousands of years of experience and wisdom. Their stares are like probing pressor beams seeking answers from the depths of my human soul.

"This day of the Ninth Moon is now in session," Loquius announces. "I will direct the meeting from my chair as Master at Arms for The Council of Elders, 9th District of Cross Over. Council member Maneethius has the table."

A frail looking Sasquatch to my right stands and proceeds to an empty chair at the head of the table. He sits but does not speak as he scrutinizes me with a soft but penetrating gaze. I do not look away. I peer back into the eyes of his soul for my own answers. What I witness is pure empathy. It is what I also feel is emanating from within myself and a binding trust simply congeals between us. I know this bond of trust is more real than any words of promise that could ever be spoken.

Maneethius stands, nods to Loquius and resumes his seat to my right.

"Council member, Rutheeus, has the table," Loquius states.

Rutheeus looks to be the youngest of the elder Sasquatch as he makes his way to the vacant chair. Though his hair is tinged in grey, he still looks muscled and vibrant. His carriage is much more challenging in stature.

"I am Rutheeus," he growls from deep within his throat. "My name means the enforcer. I've spent many, many hours with your predecessor, Ted Kaczynski. He meant well, but his mind collapsed beneath the strain and guilt he carried for the terrible state that exists in your world. Rather than tackling the responsibility to fix it, he embarked on a journey to further destroy. Since those many years, we have witnessed no change for the better amongst your kind, in fact you are on an accelerating spiral down into the chaos from which our worlds were born. You are his replacement," Rutheeus states emphatically, and points an accusing finger straight at me.

No lightning bolt explodes from his hand, but I know I am faced with an adversary like no other. I know I am at a critical crossroad in Cross Over as well as in my life as a whole, depending upon my response. Confronted with the next to impossible task of redirecting mankind conjures up images of the old TV series, Mission Impossible, where the task force is supposed to choose whether to accept the dangerous mission or not. In my mind, I am screaming *no*! Just walk away. Forget Cross Over and forget the Sasquatch. But, in my gut, I simply know that I have no choice. It was mine to begin with.

"I have already chosen to listen to the Stone Without Time," I say. "Doing otherwise would extinguish the essence of the man I am."

"Then, so be it," Rutheeus pronounces. "You are the chosen one."

6

My first meeting is with my friend Loquius. He is unusually quiet as I am served tea and some biscuits that taste like crunchy, cornbread. I eat greedily, having been famished after all the tensions associated with my Cross Over travels and the unusual formalities of the Council of Elders.

"How am I doing in your world's eyes?" I ask Loquius in an attempt to break the uncomfortable silence.

"I have cause for concerns. How to proceed in the future will mostly rely on how and what you are able to do back inside your own world," Loquius confides. "What you do here has little to no significance beyond your conversations with Rutheeus. He is a wise and powerful Sasquatch and will guide you as best as he can."

"He seems to have a bit of a chip on his shoulder," I reply.

"Many here have a chip on their shoulder. Unbeknownst to your kind, your world is looked upon as the underworld. Some wonder if you even have a conscience and think that working with denizens of the underworld will be an exercise in futility. There are many that would like to see the human race extinguished altogether for the sake of our planet earth. I am not one of them. I view such a stance as a surefire path to becoming our own executioner."

"Sort of a damned if you do and damned if you don't conundrum, I'd say," I respond.

"Yes," Loquius nods. "On the other foot, there exists the subjective reality of hope."

"I am not sure I can fill that role," I respond. "I have no power in the eyes of our so-called authorities. If I can't supply them with power and money, then I am just a cog in their huge corporate machine. I am like any other unsuspecting chattel."

"That is why you must listen to Rutheeus. I believe his mind works in tandem to your world's peculiar ways. We as a whole are a simple race, we have learned how to avoid the pitfalls of history and stay on the path that leads to a greater oneness with the creator and each other. That is all that you have lost. We know that profound ability once lived in the hearts of your predecessors and believe that it can be restored."

"I will listen," I say. "I am not enamored with man's current state of affairs either, but like I have said, I am just one man in a mass of billions. I am an insignificant number in the labyrinth of oblivion."

7

I now recognize the Sasquatch, Rutheeus, as being one of the officials that was present at the exile ceremony of Demarcus. Though Loquius was the conductor, Rutheeus had been at his elbow. He had addressed Demarkus with several of the probing questions to which the young Sasquatch had vehemently shaken his head — no.

"It is important that you know why there are Sasquatch sightings in your world," Rutheeus states. "These are Cross Over exiles. These young renegades can be dangerous and will be of no help to you nor our objectives. Demarcus and those like him have refused to abide by the mandates of never crossing over and aggressively interacting with humans. All of these exiles have been found guilty of doing so, they illegally entered your world through the same Cross Over gateways that make it possible for you and Loquius to come and go."

"People in our world have become enamored with these Sasquatch," I say. "Though I know of very few humans that have been harmed."

"That is where you are wrong. All of these exiles were guilty of snatching at least one human, sometimes more. They then brought them back here into our world. It is unfortunate and we apologize for such Sasquatch behavior."

I remember some rumors and speculations about missing hikers and campers possibly being snatched by Sasquatch. I had never taken them seriously until now.

"So, there are some humans here?" I ask incredulously.

"Possibly," Rutheeus replies. "We have never found them, only the clues and confessions of our exiles. None have ever disclosed the whereabouts of these captives."

"Why bring humans here to begin with?" I ask.

"There is a building unrest amongst the young. Your technological and industrial path, long watched but accepted by us elders, has brought much anger to the young. I am afraid they are becoming vocal and antagonistic to the dissonance of your mechanistic and social upheavals. There has been a noticeable bleed over of your hostilities and technological poisons into our world."

"Yes, Loquius has said that was why Ted Kaczynski was befriended and brought to Cross Over — to enlighten humanity on the dangers of their technological path."

"Loquius is guardian of the gateway," Rutheeus says. "He is also our ambassador as you have come to know. He has free will to cross over into your world as he sees fit. He made a mistake with Ted Kaczynski but has faith in his choice of you as our new human conduit. Loquius will always be available to you as guide and guardian within both our worlds. He will be our eyes and ears in this endeavor."

"Thank you," I reply. "His name has served me well. Loquius was a valuable password in reaching Pariseema and gaining my presence here before you and the other Elders."

"Very good. The Sasquatch will accept your help, just as you have accepted ours. Both of our worlds are approaching a volatile tipping point. It is our job to make sure that we do not have a repeat debacle and set back like that created by Ted Kaczynski. It is my goal to give you some tools and knowledge to help us resolve the unrest that is threatening to collapse both our worlds as we know them."

"I feel maybe I have overstepped my view of myself," I explain. "I have no status nor power in our world."

"You will," Rutheeus states and reaches out with his index finger.

I am compelled to extend my own and touch his.

8

I am led through a combination kitchen and dining hall, a vast library and cultural center as well as several meeting rooms before entering a labyrinth of living quarters.

I am especially attracted to and intrigued by the vast library that is stacked with row after row of parchments. On the walls there is artwork depicting Sasquatch scenes as well as colorful landscapes and wildlife. It is apparent the Sasquatch have an aptitude for the arts that I would have never dreamed.

In my spacious quarters there are quotations etched into the plastered walls. Most are in a language I do not comprehend, but there are two written in perfect English. They are both eloquent and simple enough to resonate to any consciousness with a spiritual concept of a Supreme Being. They read as follows in beautiful script:

"May the light of The Creator shine bright in your eyes; May it right the ship of hearts and minds capsized," Maneethius, The Elder.

"Be still and know that I am," God.

The last of the two quotes I remember from my mother's Bible. What strikes me is the slight alteration from third person in the Bible to first person in Cross Over. This quotation speaks volumes about the alternate viewpoints taken by two diverse races.

I can't help but be awed. I am in the presence of beings that are completely misunderstood and underestimated by human researchers and scientists. I have found myself among a culture and civilization with apparent answers to some of man's most flagrant problems. Yet as I contemplate this greatest, there are those enacting laws that would allow a Bigfoot hunting season. Such hypocrisy, and it exists totally unbeknownst to those in need.

9

In the morning I am generously cared for and once again escorted into the chambers where Rutheeus awaits my presence. He is standing over a round wooden table stacked with parchments.

"First, we shall eat breakfast," he states and motions me away from the parchment laden table onto a bench by a window. It offers a splendid view of the lake already bustling with activity. Rutheeus takes a seat on the bench right next to me. I can feel an intense heat emanating from his towering body.

"I hope you've found your quarters satisfactory," he queries, then gestures to a young Sasquatch holding a tray of fresh fruits.

Set before me, are huge blackberries as well as strawberries mixed with melons heaped in coconut shells. I am also offered a cup into which the youngster respectfully pours a deep, lavender colored tea.

"My quarters were splendid," I reply to Rutheeus. "I was very impressed by the work of your artists."

"Please, help yourself to the fruits," he says. "That was my son, Severius, he will return shortly with a fresh batch of baka to go with your tea."

"Thank you," I tell the elder.

"As for our artists, they are deeply treasured," Rutheeus extols. "They are the divine nurturers and guardians of the sanctity and beauty of life."

"Our artists are also revered… well, were revered at one time," I modify. "Now, it seems they are popularized and idolized for political agendas and degrading behaviors instead of cultural art."

Rutheeus' eyes lock on mine and I can feel a softer transformation somewhere deep in his perspective.

"It is essential for man to find his soul," he intones quietly, and continues to hold my gaze.

Under other circumstances, I could have easily mistaken his intensity for a threat.

Then Rutheeus smiles for the first time and pops a fresh blackberry into his mouth. He motions with a big hand that I should follow suit.

The fruit is bursting with intense flavors and succulent juices. The baka reminds me of the Jewish treat I have known of as Halva. It is heavenly nutty, musty and sweet.

"It is delicious," I tell Rutheeus.

Rutheeus nods, and like my time spent with Loquius and his family, Rutheeus raises his arms and gives an intonation of thanks to the life affirming sustenance of which we are blessed. He then helps himself to more fruit, tastes the baka and nods pleasurably.

I smile and nod in agreement as I take a sip of tea. I find it very complimentary to the fruits, rich with cherries and a hint of chocolate.

As we eat, we are enveloped in a cocoon of relaxed silence. I am filled with a sense of joy and brotherhood. What-ever shoulder chip I had felt Rutheeus had been carrying, had dissipated over a bountiful breakfast in Cross Over.

10

Severius pours us a final cup of tea and excuses himself with a slight bow.

"I hope we can help and trust each other," Rutheeus originates, and lays a huge hand on my shoulder. "I am a bit of a skeptic and have less faith in the future of your race than some of the other Elders. I am younger, and what some of them might call "rash." It was Loquius that convinced me you are deserving of being here and given a chance to prove me wrong. And now that I have sat beside you, I have come to the point where I agree."

I can feel the weight of his hand and know its strength could crush me in an instant if the desire to do so was there. As it is, its compassion is a moment of clarity and a poignant re-ignition of a purpose long idling in my soul.

"My trust is granted," I say without reservation.

"I offer my trust as well," Rutheeus replies and once again extends his index finger to touch mine. When our fingers meet, it is a heartwarming energy that passes between us. I am certain our trust now holds reality instead of some abstract idea.

We both nod and smile.

"Please," Rutheeus says and gestures toward the table with the pile of parchments. "I have prepared a few things for your benefit."

At the table there is a small pile of human sized papers lying beside the large parchments that I had noticed upon entering the chamber. Rutheeus picks up the small pile and leafs through them quickly before handing them over to me.

"These are yours to keep," he tells me. "I would like you to look at them now and then continue to study them for the future of your world."

I accept the parchments, all told there appears to be about twenty pages. The paper is coarse and yellowed.

"I am prepared to answer any questions you may have," Rutheeeus states and ushers me to a chair near the table. He then sits down before the stack of large parchments and begins to write.

The top paper of my stack is entitled: *The Secret of Time.*

There are no other words on the page, only a drawing of a six-pointed star with a colored-in hexagon that is created by the base of each of the star's points.

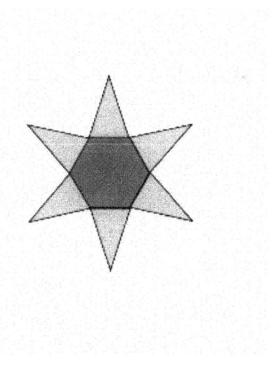

The second page is entitled: *The is of what is is is.*

Again there are no words. It contains a beautiful painting of planet earth floating in a galactic sea.

And that is how all the pages go. Each has a profound title defined by a simple picture of that page's concept. Some I immediately grasp while others are beyond my limited comprehension.

I raise my hand.

Rutheeus peers up at me and nods.

"The first page," I say. "I don't understand its meaning."

"It is the law of how our worlds can occupy the same space. In other words, space is not made of time. Space is not bound, it is limitless, so it exists outside the realm of time. That is what you humans have forgotten. You are a race lost in time."

His description wrestles and gnaws at some deep understanding, but still remains, illusive.

"I cannot deny both our worlds exist," I say. "They are quite different but yet the same."

"Very good, the importance is not in the idea, the importance is in the fact that you are the source of both space and time within your own personal world. You are one source of what materializes and persists in the world around you. You can change existence, or in other words, space and time, by simply changing your mind, and that is the secret of time. The ultimate test lies in your ability to change the minds of others."

11

After what seems like hours lost in the parchments, my head is spinning. I have grasped as many of the Sasquatch concepts as my mind can digest in one sitting. The final page in the stack states: *Life is not divisible into itself.* The picture that's associated with this concept is once again a painting of planet earth floating in a galactic sea. The exact same painting that has described more than one concept from the parchments. I am sure it probably has more significance than I can fathom, but the gist of that significance means to me that life is a whole. It means planet earth is a living being unto itself. It is not divisible if it is to remain healthy and whole. You cannot destroy any of its parts unless you want problems with its other parts. You pollute the air, you pollute everything. You poison the bugs, you poison yourself.

"Good enough," I say to Rutheeus. "I am satisfied in my knowledge of Sasquatch philosophy."

"I am pleased," Rutheeus says. "You are much like Ted. The major difference between you and he is that what you have learned does not make you angry. It motivates you and that is a major difference. As for philosophy, that is not my intention, you are simply perceiving our creational truths. Truth is the mother of life, not philosophy."

"Understood," I say. "We try to adhere to similar precepts in our world."

"The final lesson for today is in this bag," Rutheeus says, and hands it to me.

He had picked it up and handed it over like it was a bag of yarn, but to me it was surprisingly heavy. Upon inspection, it contains one large sack and two smaller sacks of seed as well as a tangle of roots and something that looks strangely like chewing tobacco.

"Seeds and roots are the beginning of change. Plant them and grow them and your world will evolve for the better. They are magic."

"Thank you, I will do as you wish, but I am afraid winter is near and they will have to wait until spring."

"We shall see. Go home, apply what you have learned and keep learning— and remember it is you that is the creator of time and space."

"What is this?" I ask, holding up the stuff that looks like RedMan Chewing tobacco.

"We once allowed humans to travel here." Rutheeus explains. "They were adept in their use of the Stone Without Time. They came on vision quests. We welcomed them and they took much knowledge of our world back with them to apply in yours. They were the Mida."

I finger the lapis stone in my pocket and get a strong image of my friend Tecumseh.

"Consider it a gift that will help you create time in your world," Rutheeus says. "It's my gesture of trust from the Sasquatch."

"I am thankful," I respond. "But what is it?"

"It has a voice, listen to it. It will speak when the time comes, and you will know."

I sense that is all I am going to get from Rutheeus. I am struck with an understanding our meeting is over. I reach with my index finger and once again receive a tremendous influx of empathy when his finger touches the tip of mine.

12

The sun tells me it is midmorning. I am basking in its warmth on the stairs at the entrance to the rotunda. I feel invigorated. Lake Pariseema is sparkling and I can see Sasquatch with long cane poles fishing from their rafts. Others are traversing the lake in dugouts that glide through the water like kayaks. Several transport rafts are cued to unload their goods at the landing docks. It is such a glorious day devoid of the looming stresses and responsibilities outside the realm of Cross Over.

"I am told that Rutheeus was pleased with your meeting," Loquius says as he sidles up next to me on the stairs.

I immediately rise and greet my huge friend with my index finger. I have become enamored with this intimate greeting and acknowledgement.

"It went well," I state and show the bag with its plethora of gifts given to me by Rutheeus.

Loquius nods. "Your world deserves them," he exclaims. "And now it is my duty to get you back to that place you call humanity."

"Yes, it seems I have been entrusted with much to do. It also seems I have been away for weeks instead of just a couple of days."

Loquius gives me his wry smile. "Don't let time fool you. It is full of deception and trickery. Being in the present is the essence of successful living. And now we will travel in a pirogue. It is a dugout like those you can see on the lake. It is light and swift like the wolf that will lead you later on today. Come."

We descend the stairs to the docking area where Loquius has assembled a small pile of gear. The pirogue is about nine feet long and four feet wide. His two-bladed paddle is almost as long as the boat.

Loquius single-handedly slips the pirogue into the water and stows our gear. I am directed to sit on a mat about three feet from the craft's stern. For such a light and narrow craft, the pirogue is surprisingly stable even when Loquius' full weight bears down while he moves to a flat area mid-ship. It is from there he dips his paddle and muscles us swiftly out into and across Lake Pariseema. From there we move swiftly down the Cross Over version of the Au Sable River.

I am impressed once again by the strength and fluidity of these strange and beautiful creatures. Watching Loquius is like watching a panther doing ballet. Sounds strange, but that is my image of Sasquatch grace.

Loquius eventually glides us ashore at a sandy beach and ties us off. He hands me my backpack as I am greeted by a Sasquatch no taller than myself.

"This young fellow will get you back to Big Creek," Loquius informs me and smiles. "So, travel well my friend, I will find you another day on the ridge beside Big Creek."

I am unexpectedly overcome by loss. I am truly sad to say goodbye.

"Soon, my friend," I manage and reach out with my index finger. There is no hint of sadness in Loquius' eyes, only joy that I receive in a vibrant starburst from his touch.

As Loquius departs, the young Sasquatch beckons to me and turns away, heading up the path away from the river. I fall in step behind him and labor up the switchbacks that lead us out of the river's steep ravine. At the top, the land levels out and the forest descends gently into the green valley that I recognize from my earlier trek into Cross Over.

Frenzied yips and barks are emanating from under a tree where I notice two huge wolves fidgeting impatiently. My young guide whistles softly and the wolves prance and bound to his side. He says something in Sasquatch whereby the wolves calm, immediately sit on their haunches and put their full attention on me. One tilts its head and whines softly, the other bares its teeth.

The young Sasquatch looks at me and taps his chest. "Cavinus," he says. He points to the wolf with bared teeth, "Dagre." He then points to the wolf with its eager whine. "Peeba," he says.

Cavinus then hefts my backpack over his shoulder, grips a wooden handhold at the side of Dagre's neck, steps into a belly stirrup and mounts Dagre.

Peeba whines and scuttles up to me, belly to the ground. Her cold nose nuzzles my hand. Her big eyes are soft and attentive. But even lying down the huge animal is intimidating.

Cavinus nods.

I reluctantly get a good grip with hand and foot and follow Cavinus's example by mounting the wolf's back. The makeshift straps and seat put me in a prone position similar to a jockey on a racehorse. I can feel that the saddle adjusts by an ingenious design of weight and tension, and by doing so feels quite secure. I am confident that I won't fall off.

Cavinus clicks his teeth.

Peeba stands, momentarily sidesteps as if to test our connection and seemingly satisfied takes off like a bullet.

I am bombarded by a rush of exhilarating sensations. I can feel the intricate workings of my wolf's bone and muscle as the trees fly by in a blur. The wind cascades over me like a waterfall. The multi-layered smells of greenery and flowers are bold and intoxicating beyond belief. *Please Santa*, I think, *bring me a Cross Over wolf for Christmas!*

I have ridden many animals: horses, donkeys, mules, bulls and even a camel. Those rides were like the merry-go-round at the county fair, riding Peeba is like the loop-to-loop rocket to the moon.

All too soon it is over. Peeba is once again belly to the ground as Cavinus places my backpack at his feet. I dismount the wolf, shaking. I have a case of sea legs and a disorientation that makes me wobble like a drunk.

Cavinus watches me with amusement and nods, then remounts Dagre. Peeba yips and gives me a quick kiss, then in a flash they are gone. I am left standing alone in the forest beside the creek where I had witnessed to Damarcus being exiled.

The weather is very pleasant, but I wonder what might be in store on the other side. I'd hate to arrive near Lewiston soaking wet in a snowstorm. It is late October in Michigan and nothing is out of the question. My car is parked a couple miles from my Big Creek location, far enough that I could freeze to death should I be wet and unable to get dried out before reaching my destination. Concerned, I dig into my pack. To my relief, my matches are still dry and securely ensconced in their plastic tube and baggie. I breathe a sigh of relief and relax into to my rubbery legs. What a ride!

Standing so close to the rip between our two universes, I can feel The Stone Without Time warming and beckoning from within my pocket. I quickly pull it out, curious to view what vision it might have in store for me.

Instead of pointing into the water, the stone shows me an image of a huge tree located somewhere north along the stream. Most of the trees in that direction are large, but the one pictured in the stone is conspicuously leaning out over the water with its roots, half exposed. I follow the stone's lead and it only takes me a few minutes before I find the vision's exact tree. I notice immediately that it has been struck by lightning, leaving a gaping wound at the base of its trunk. The opening is charred black and more than large enough for me to enter standing up.

Inside the tree the telltale smell of ozone is stronger than ever. There is nothing to see but blackness. I reach out with my arm to test if I can touch the other side and find nothing there but black space.

I have always prided myself for having superb night vision, in fact I used to earn extra income taking RV campers on night excursions into the starlit landscapes near the campground in the town of Mio. So my ability to see in the dark is beyond reproach, but the darkness I am experiencing inside the burned-out tree has collapsed heavily around me. I am completely blind. I have to grope with my hands in search for anything solid, but with each step all I encounter is more and more empty space. This emptiness is beyond reasoning and comprehension. I find it spooky, disorienting and somewhat claustrophobic, and I willingly admit to having a moment of panic as I turn around and attempt to retrace my steps in order to find my way back and out of the entrance. It is gone.

I am lost in a black hole between two worlds, apparently in that nowhere space where Tecumseh said he may not be able to find me in order to bring me back. The one thing I find comforting is that my feet are still on solid ground, that the empty space does not apparently extend all dimensionally or I would be in a state like an astronaut floating untethered in outer space.

I take several deep breaths and close my eyes. As I relax, I take cognizance of my own thoughts and pictures in my mind. Loquius had explained that we can always view what we choose to mock-up inside the sanctuary of our own minds, a place where the movies can be rewound and fast forwarded as we please. The trick is to put the right pictures there to view, and I am in need of something soothing and bright to cancel out the darkness.

I focus very hard on what I'd like to see in my immediate future. I am warmed by a vision of the sun dappling the lush forest floor. I see the floor covered in a carpet of orange and gold autumn leaves. They are sprinkled everywhere. I can see the shadows flicker and dance as the wind rustles the branches of the leafless poplars and birches next to the creek.

As the pictures grow clear, my other senses kick in as well. I can smell the rich organic fragrances of the forest. The first thing I hear are some perturbed Blue Jays that always seem to be in a state of watchful alarm when a human is about. A squirrel catches my presence and scolds me raucously. I feel the temperature suddenly drop about twenty degrees.

The first thing I see when I open my eyes is Tecumseh. His creviced and smiling face is only a few feet away from mine. He is standing there as sure as the day is filled with sunshine in a colorful display of autumn.

"I have been searching everywhere for you, my friend," he exclaims and spreads his arms in a welcoming gesture of joy and affection.

We hug. There is no doubt that I have managed to visualize my way out of Cross Over and back to Lewiston or maybe Tecumseh was able to bring me back after all.

15

Tecumseh does not own a car. He has an old Indian motorcycle that runs on prayers and his constant tinkering.

"I'll follow you back to your place," I tell him and throw my backpack into the backseat of my Mazda where everything seems to be in order. My phone, gun and ammunition are all still safely sequestered in the floorboard toolbox designed for that specific purpose.

Tecumseh's bike roars to life, does a donut and zips up the two-lane trail out of the woods.

I feel both elated and in shock, elated to be home, but in shock in having learned that I have apparently been gone for two weeks instead of my vivid recollection of having only been gone a couple of days.

Tecumseh said there has been some worry and upset bubbling up at home. Two weeks is way beyond my wife and I's agreed upon behavior. Fortunately, she is well grounded and was able to keep her anger in check, she contacted Tecumseh for consultation instead of reaching in a panic to the local police. Tecumseh reassured her I was simply away on a vision quest and would return as soon as I was able. When Tecumseh and I finally appeared before each other, he had been searching for signs of my whereabouts for several days. He said he had even begun to worry and wonder himself, if I would successfully navigate my way back from Cross Over. I don't know how, but I apparently spent way longer wandering around in the dark between worlds than I have memories to recollect.

Tecumseh's town of Comins is a tiny place, it has a post office, a bar and a convenience store, not much else. Tecumseh lives in a trailer with a few acres bordering state land on the edge of town, and that is where he offers me a meal of smoked salmon, crackers and a cold ginger ale.

I am still somewhat shocked and reluctant to join the human race, so the respite before dealing with my domestic issues is a welcoming gesture. The smoked salmon is delicious with a hardened coating of brown sugar, maple syrup, pepper and salt.

"Tell me," Tecumseh beckons. "How are my brethren the Chiha Tanka doing in that world of theirs?"

"Hang on," I say, as I hustle back to the car to retrieve my bag with the Sasquatch parchments, seeds and roots. On my return, to help alleviate any further worry and concern, I pause and call my wife. I apologize with a sincere promise to be home in an hour.

"Check this out," I tell Tecumseh and hand over the first of the Sasquatch parchments.

Tecumseh looks it over. "It's a teepee," he says. "If you take the star points and fold them all vertically, you have a perfect teepee."

"Hmmm," I respond. "Now that you mention it, I can see that. What do you make of the caption?"

"The Secret of Time," Tecumseh mouths and ponders. "A teepee is sister to The Stone Without Time. It's a spirit catcher. It preserves our memories and passes them down. I have claimed the memories of my father and my mother, and the memories of their fathers and mothers before them. Time does not exist in the realm of the spirit."

"You never fail to enlighten me, my friend. That's what the world is like over there, timeless. Somehow preserved. It's like a step back and a step forward at the same time. Cross Over exists somewhere beyond man's everyday concept or perception of reality. There are forces in this universe we truly do not understand."

"And you have become the conduit and messenger," Tecumseh says with certainty. "You are Mida, a Chippewa out of time, like me."

16

With the Cross Over encounters with the Sasquatch behind me, I am spending some time staying close to home, hanging around my computer. I have been more than willing to be at my wife's beck and call for domestic activities and help. It's the least I can do. She has forgiven me.

On the depressing side, I have returned home to another round of viral shutdowns by the government. The governor has developed a morbid love affair with imposing unconstitutional edicts on Michigan's populace by stopping everybody from having any meaningful travel or social contact. Many businesses are shut down. I am thankful local authorities and some businesses have the will to mostly ignore her and remain open, for if this mask wearing and social distancing becomes what people are willing to deem acceptable as the new normal, the Sasquatch and I will be confronted with a near impossible task out in front of us.

I don't have time to be depressed and open Google to do a search.

Ted Kaczynski and his Unabomber Manifesto is 35,000 words long. It is nothing like what I would have expected it to be, since Ted Kaczynski was demonized and portrayed in the media as one of the world's most radical leftists, an anarchist, and a domestic terrorist of the first degree.

Not true.

Except for his misguided way of getting his point across, his words tell me he was the exact opposite of that leftist portrayal. He was far from an anarchist. He was far from a dummy who would belong to a terrorist group like Antifa. I can see he was highly intelligent with intuitive skills and reasoning far beyond Harvard's boxes of intellectuals.

It is obvious that Ted Kaczynski is an individualist and a free thinker. I have to conclude that he became cornered and saw no other avenue for disseminating his Cross Over knowledge other than through violence and threats of further violence. His targets were clearly defined and carried out with precision to gain attention in order to produce an effect.

Ted Kaczynski was willing to endanger and sacrifice his own well-being and freedom to get his message out to an uninformed world. Struggling with conflicting feelings, I find his manifesto message is a message highly relevant to the state of our world at this time.

Kaczynski wrote extensively on the downfalls and dehumanizing effects of a demoralized and technological society. He'd found agreement not from his colleagues at places like Harvard, but from the Sasquatch of Cross Over. What he found there was a way of life in harmony and symbiosis with all other life. He found a profound sense of simplicity that he believed could heal man's overly materialized and techno-ravaged soul.

I personally know my social and ethical boundaries. I am not an anarchist or a politician. I am simply a messenger for the Sasquatch as purported by my friend Tecumseh. I have certainly become emotionally and intellectually invested in the Bigfoot's way of life. I admire these creatures' desire to help planet earth. I believe their intent is honest and well-reasoned.

That is my sermon and soul searching for today. My next internet search is to discover what I might find and achieve through the sacks of seed, roots and other goodies I have been lucky enough to bring back from the magical land of Cross Over.

17

I am discovering a few interesting things on the internet. I have found that I have returned from the Sasquatch with two sacks of kenaf seeds, and another Google search has led me quite miraculously to a kenaf researcher just down the road in Onaway, Michigan. I have also found a state of the art processor of hemp, and possibly kenaf in Gladwin, Michigan. This I find very intriguing, because it aligns with the third Sasquatch parchment that I am holding in my hands, it states: **Nothing is by Coincidence**. This is an intriguing truth so easily dismissed by the weak minded because responsibility for such an all-consuming statement is hard to fathom. The parchment picture associated with this concept is an empty circle, or a zero.

I already have an intuitive grasp of this concept. I have studied the parchments and it means full responsibility equals zero. In the language of math, it is the equivalent of the denominator that cancels out every numerator by being equal. In other words, taking full responsibility leaves absolutely nothing to which justifications or lies can attach themselves. What remains is simply the truth. **Nothing is by Coincidence**.

Onaway, Michigan is the home of Kenaf Partners USA, a website loaded with information about the valuable Sasquatch kenaf seeds I have brought back from Cross Over. Unbeknownst to me, kenaf has been building a foothold in nearby Onaway for several years. The word Onaway itself is an American Indian term meaning "The Awakening." I am certain that it is no accident that the hub for disseminating kenaf books, seeds and other information on regenerative agriculture happens to be located in Onaway, right next door to a Sasquatch portal to Cross Over.

The processing center in Gladwin is just icing on the cake. I can see that I am perfectly located in the eye of the "The Awakening."

I am wrenched from my deep thoughts by the rumbling sound of Tecumseh's motorcycle roaring up the driveway. I dog paddle to the surface of reality and drop my research. I quickly slip on my shoes and hustle out the front door to meet him.

It must be something important, I'm thinking. I know my friend. He wouldn't get all bundled-up to venture out on such a bitter cold day just to ride his bike. The temperature is in the mid-teens with the first flakes of snow fluttering in the wintery wind.

"What's up Tecumseh?" I call out over the chugga-chugga of his machine.

He throttles down and removes his gloves and googles.

"We've got a Mida problem, my friend. Buddy Decker is on the war path. He's forming up a vigilante posse to go after one of your Sasquatch friends who he says busted up his cabin."

"Buddy Decker?" I raise my arms in confusion.

"Ex-deputy Sheriff from Bay City. Him and his brother bought the old 405 Camp over there abutting

Big Creek State land of which you are so fond. Said he saw a Bigfoot hightailing it for the trees when he arrived to open the camp for deer season."

"I'll be darned," I say. "I'll bet the poker pot that it's a Squatch by the name of Demarcus. He was looking for a fight with me before my friend Loquius intervened just prior to my first trip into Cross Over. Demarcus is a rebellious sort, just recently exiled from Cross Over for supposedly kidnapping humans."

"Now he's earned himself a bounty on his head. Decker was in the party store in Comins, talking up young Jeff Davies to get his buddies together. Decker wants them to come on out and flush-drive the woods while he and his brother set up in their tree stands along Big Creek with their rifles."

"Give me a minute to get dressed and collect my gear," I say. "We'll head on down there in the truck, no need for the bike. You got your gun?"

"More than one," Tecumseh admits.

I decide to get my Beretta out of the car and grab my lever action 30-30 rifle. The rifle is light and short, great for navigating through the woods.

"It'd be nice to beat those guys out there," I say. "But if they happen to be there already, it might even be a good idea to drive up to their camp and volunteer for his posse. That way we can keep an eye on things, kind of mess with the works if we need to."

"You decide," Tecumseh shrugs. "I'll have your back either way."

18

When we get on the road and drive the 405 to the Decker Camp road entrance, we find the camp chain securely across the road and padlocked. No sign of activity.

"I'd say the posse is still forming," Tecumseh reasons. "Otherwise the chain would be down and there would be plenty of fresh tire tracks."

"I agree, we've beaten the posse, so let's park at my usual spot and walk in along the ridge. I think I know where one of Decker's tree stands is located. I ran into it awhile back on my way to meeting Loquius."

Tecumseh pulls his 30.06 out of its case, an old service model. It's a heavy gun, but powerful and accurate at long range. He loads his clip as I get us down the road and park in a grove of cedars.

"One thing," I say. "We're out here to stop a senseless killing. Demarcus is just a homeless teenager. A pretty ticked off Sasquatch no doubt, so we need to be careful but prudent. If we find him, I'll attempt to reason with him, but like you indicated earlier, if things go south, you need to be ready to have my back. Shoot to scare him if you have to and if it escalates beyond that, well, I trust your warrior judgement."

Tecumseh gives me a thumbs up and gets out of the truck. I do the same and load my 30-30. I put the Beretta in a holster on my hip.

"Ready, my friend?" I ask.

"Just a little paint," Tecumseh says and uncaps a tin of brown shoe polish. He traces several streaks across his cheeks and forehead. "You should do the same," he tells me.

I chuckle and take the offered tin. No harm in a little war paint to camouflage my shiny white face.

19

After several days at home in the office, it is a joy to be back in the woods. Even though the wind chill is probably close to five degrees I feel warmed by the activity.

"What's the plan?" Tecumseh asks.

"I'll go out front, you shadow me. The thing about these Sasquatch is that they like to sneak up on you. They remind me of you Chippewas.

Tecumseh chuckles and nods his head.

As I make my way above the creek bottom, I keep my eye out for any signs of Demarcus. Tecumseh is nowhere to be seen nor heard, though I know he is there somewhere close by. At the tree stand of which I assume is the work of Buddy Decker, I find nothing unusual. There are frozen apples in a pile that have been pawed through by deer and probably a porcupine or two.

By the time I reach the ridge near the Cross Over portal, I have seen little to indicate that Demarcus has been around. Not sure how to proceed, I take off a glove, insert two fingers in my mouth and create a short shrill whistle. Tecumseh walks out of a clump of cedars some fifteen yards away toward the creek.

"Any sign of the Squatch?" I whisper.

Nothing at all he indicates by swiping a finger across his throat.

"I'm surprised," I acknowledge quietly. "Where is Decker's cabin from here?"

Tecumseh points east and a little north from our location. He then holds his hands about six inches apart indicating about a half mile away.

"You lead the way," I indicate. "I'll shadow you this time. If you catch wind of Decker and his posse, hunker down and give me a whistle."

Tecumseh silently moves off in the direction of the camp. I follow in his shadow.

I'm not great, but I'm pretty good at playing Daniel Boone. I have been moving with stealth through the woods ever since my father taught me how to hunt as a child. It is a dance of feel and instinct honed to a razor's edge. Tecumseh is the best.

A quarter of a mile in, I hear the soft whistle. Tecumseh is crouched behind a small blue spruce and is motioning me to stay low. I duck and slip up next to him.

"Blue Jays," he whispers.

Sure enough, I can hear them warning one another of an interloper and I am pretty certain it is not us. If it was, there'd be one scolding us from a tree right above our heads.

"There," he says and points.

I catch a glimpse of a red hat bobbing like a wild turkey in some trees about thirty yards away. The hat is closely followed by a large dark shadow.

"Chiha Tanka," Tecumseh whispers.

"Interesting," I say. "I wond...."

I am cut off by a muffled cry and a disconcerting thud.

Both Tecumseh and I are immediately on our feet and scurrying towards the commotion.

20

A thundering gunshot reverberates through the forest, followed by a shriek of pain. It is definitely a human cry and not from the Sasquatch.

When we clear the small rise and gain visibility of the chaos, Decker or whoever the man in the red hat happens to be, (I assume it is Decker) is seated on the ground with a bloody face. He's attempting to scuttle backwards up the ravine's slope, but unable to get a foothold in all the wet leaves.

Demarcus is towering over the man with a scowl and has a solid grip on the guy's gun. I can see Demarcus' huge hands and arms straining with pressure and force on the weapon's barrel. With his tense muscles vibrating, the Sasquatch slowly bends the gun into a parabola.

Decker is bug-eyed and whimpering like a dog. He's still trying to back up the slippery slope away from the Bigfoot when Demarcus lets out an earsplitting screech. He then sends the useless gun spinning deep into the trees.

"Move Decker!" I yell. "Move!"

Decker finally turns his body away from Demarcus and begins using his hands to find purchase on some small shrubs. He is moving up the slope when one of Damarcus's huge mitts swipes and catches an ankle. Decker is yanked into the air like a ragdoll, where he hangs upside down, face to face with Demarcus' roiling eyes.

"Demarcus!" I scream at the top of my lungs. "Put him down!"

Demarcus' head spins and looks at us. Tecumseh and I are about thirty feet away atop the small rise. The Sasquatch looks from me to Decker, back and forth, almost like somebody weighing the idea that a bird in hand is worth two in the bush. I get a bloody vision of Demarcus grabbing Decker's other leg and splitting him in half like a wishbone from a Christmas Turkey.

"Demarcus!" I scream again. "Put the man down!"

Demarcus's breaks his attention from Decker and turns it fully onto me, his body vibrating with a mass of pent-up rage. His grip on Decker's ankle suddenly relaxes and Decker plummets to the ground with another loud grunt and cry in pain.

"Don't do it Demarcus," I warn. "We are here to help you, not harm."

Demarcus lets loose with another piercing wail.

"Shoot him! For Christ sake, shoot him!" Decker yells up at us.

Tecumseh has the 30.06 propped on a tree branch and zeroed in.

"Not yet my friend," I whisper.

"Decker, get your ass out of there!" I call forcefully but calmly, all the while keeping my attention firmly on the Bigfoot.

"Demarcus," I say. "My friend here has a big gun pointed at your heart. Don't be a fool."

There is a discernible change in vibration as if the forest around us has been holding its breath. It sighs and a cold breeze tickles my neck. I shiver as Demarcus's big form wavers and seems to shrink to nothing before our eyes, then he is gone.

21

"What the Hell!"

I turn my attention to the strange voice behind me. Decker's bloody face is there, focused on Tecumseh who is now cradling his 30.06 in a position of ease.

"You had a perfect shot, you fool. Why didn't you pull the trigger?"

"No need," Tecumseh responds." He let you go and was unarmed."

"He was going to kill me," Decker seethes.

"Maybe," Tecumseh says in a soft voice. "Maybe not. It was you who was going to kill him is the actual truth of the matter."

"Hell, yes I would!"

"There lies the reason of why I didn't shoot. Take solace in the fact that I wasn't forced to shoot you for attempting to shoot him."

I could see Decker's brain trying to chew on the strange reasoning being offered up by a weathered Indian with a powerful gaze and war paint on his face.

"I would count your graces, Decker. You are alive. Bigfoot didn't get you, nor did my friend here with the rifle. I should think you would be happy to walk away with just a little blood on your face," I broach.

Now he is frowning at me with a glazed look. I can see he is a pretty dense guy, certainly not used to being chastised by anyone in the middle of the forest.

"You're an ex-cop. You know the line," I add.

That seems to sink in. The frown relaxes as he folds his lips inward in a small gesture of relinquishment.

"We'll take care of the Sasquatch," I say. "I don't know why he bothered your cabin, but I assume it was you that somehow instigated it, am I right?"

"Who are you people?" Decker asks defensively.

"Friends," I say. "None of this goes anywhere. You just head on back to your cabin, disband your posse and it will all be forgotten."

"Couple of spooks, aren't you?" he says shaking his head. "I have no desire to pick a fight with the FBI. But be fair warned, you stay the hell off of our land. You hear me? We can get a little trigger itchy when it comes to trespassers."

I nod.

At that, Decker dismisses us, turns on his heels and stomps awkwardly back toward his camp.

22

"What's the plan now, boss?" Tecumseh asks me.

"I still think I am going to have to try and reason with Demarcus or we really will have the FBI breathing down our necks around here. I think we are safe with Decker, but if that Bigfoot starts to terrorize some other people, things could get out of hand really quick."

"I don't like the sound of that g-word. You know how we Chippewas feel about your so called government."

"You know I agree with you; so, we need to find this dude and keep a lid on what's going on in these here woods."

"From the looks of it, I'd say he's been holing up in the swamp. You have any idea what its like in there?"

"Sort of. This time of the year is way better than spring or summer. A lot less water and no bugs and snakes. Just hard going."

"Agreed."

"Well, let's go take a look," I propose.

Swamp water, for whatever reason is somewhat freeze resistant. Being it is the first real cold day of the winter, most of the water only has a skim coat of ice. The positive take from that hampering aspect, is that Tecumseh could follow a weasel if need be, let alone a Sasquatch under these obvious tracking conditions.

"Here," Tecumseh says.

Sure enough, Demarcus has entered the swamp not a hundred yards down the ridge line. The tracks are heavy footed and easy to follow in the muddy ice breaks.

A short distance into the crusted swamp water, we find Demarcus has turned right and is angling back along the ridge.

"Tell you what," I say to Tecumseh. "I'll head back out and walk the ridge line to see if he comes back on out. I can make much better time in the open. You follow him and if he turns deeper give me a whistle and I'll catch up. I'll do the same if his tracks come out into the clear."

Tecumseh nods and quickly heads into the wake of Demarcus' trail.

The ridge is a breeze compared to sloshing through the muck and ice. It takes me little time to get far enough down the ridge to where I worry a whistle from Tecumseh may go unheard. I have found no sign of Demarcus leaving the swamp. So, after a short rest and no whistle, I continue.

The Big Creek Ridge descends into a hellhole called Dead Horse Sink. Its only inhabitants are various reptiles and long-necked birds. I can't even imagine Demarcus sloshing his way through such an inhospitable environment. I expect to see his tracks reappear along the edge of the swamp.

When I fail to find any sign of the Bigfoot, I am quite baffled as to his reasoning. I suppose he'd at least have the advantage of being able to poke his head up out of the long grasses and scrub willows to see where he was headed, but Tecumseh and I, we're as done as done can be. My Indian friend, for reasons of the past, would never even consider entering the sink. Some of his not too distant relatives perished there when their horses got bogged down in the black muck and they were slaughtered by the British Army. That was at the end of Michigan's Native American Rebellion of 1763. Thus the swamp's ill begotten name.

There's a short burst of whistles before Tecumseh rises like a Zombie from the dead. He's covered in grunge and a facial scowl from ear to ear.

I expect Demarcus will surface again in the not too distant future, but in the meantime, I'll have to get busy putting my mind to the role as a messenger for Rutheeus. I have more of the parchments to decipher. I need to figure out what the heck the chewing tobacco like substance from my Cross Over bag is composed of and what it might be used for. I also have some unidentified roots from that same bag. How is this stuff going to change the trajectory of man's thinking ignorer to save the human race?

What I know so far is that I have two bags of kenaf seeds. Kenaf might be the answer to regenerating our depleted soils, possibly to all kinds of human nutrition and animal feeds, to cheap housing and all sorts of other valuable products. I am excited about meeting the men behind the kenaf research that is occurring just down the road in the villages of Onaway and Gladwin.

Tecumseh approaches me and shakes his head no.

"His tracks disappeared into the sink," he tells me. "I cannot go into the land of the cursed. I can hear the screams and smell the blood of my ancestors."

"I understand, my friend, I have no desire to chase after a ghost. I think he has a secret entrance back into Cross Over somewhere in the Sink, I believe it is for whatever kidnapping purposes he and his renegade friends have devised. As for now, I think he is gone."

Tecumseh acknowledges with a shake of his head and touches my arm.

"You need to be careful, my friend. There are many stories about the Chiha Tanka. Many are good, but some not so good."

I feel a great warmth for the man and nod in acknowledgement. The silence around us is complete, but as we turn to walk up the slope of the ridge, an unmistakable screeching roar rises out of the depths of Dead Horse Sink.

The End

Conversations With Sasquatch will be continued in Book 3, *The Awakening*.   Once again, you may follow along as I write *Conversations With Sasquatch, The Awakening* online on my website: www.conversationswithsasquatch.com

Conversations
with
Sasquatch

The Encounter
Richard Rensberry

The first book in the Conversations With Sasquatch
series is *The Encounter*

It is available on Amazon and in my online store at:
store.booksmakebooms.com

Glossary of Terms

abhor*- regard with disgust or hate

abject*- experienced to the maximum degree

accosted*- approach and address boldly or
aggressively

adrenalin*- hormone secretion from the adrenal
glands for extra power and energy in times of fear,
excitement, etc.

Al Kaline*- Detroit Tigers baseball power hitter that
batted fourth in the lineup back in the 1960's and 70's.
He had many homers during that era

Anishinaabe*- Native Americans, ancestors of the
Chippewa

attuned*- in harmony or agreement

auras*- the electrical and emotional emanations
surrounding a body

auspicious*- a good omen, successful or prosperous

barred*- imprisoned behind bars

beefsteaks*- an edible mushroom similar to the morel but much larger and irregular of shape, reddish brown in color

befuddled*- confused

Beretta*- a brand of handgun

brethren*- archaic plural of brother

cache*- a hidden collection or store of items of some type

chiha tanka*- Native American name for Sasquatch or Big Foot

circumnavigating*- going around

conducive*- useful and fitting

conspiratorially*- a planning and acting together

crepuscule*- the hour of twilight

cut*- baseball bat swing

deftly*- skillfully

delusional*- seeing things that aren't there or real

disheveled*- disarranged and untidy

DNR*- Department of Natural Resources

edible*- fit to be eaten

effused*- poured out or forth

egress*- action of going out or leaving

encroached*- trespass or intrude

epitome*- having the characteristics or quality of the whole.

Ernie Harrell*- Radio announcer for the Detroit Tigers

ewer*- pitcher-like container for holding liquids

fingers*- here means the elongated leaves

flap-trap*- a lot of talk

Giigooh na*- Native American name for big fish

grimace- facial expression of pain of dislike

guttural*- from deep in the body

hackles*- neck hairs

hallucinated- saw things that were not actually there

harboring*- holding in

heft*- to lift

hookah*- many tubed smoking pipe

idiosyncrasies*- any personal peculiarity or mannerism

incoherently*- not understandable, gibberish

inexplicably*- unexplainable, not understood

juking*- dodging and darting

kenaf*- a variety of hibiscus plant valuable for its fibers and thousands of other useful properties

makwa*- Native American name for black bear

mangy*- shabby and filthy

manifesto*- a public declaration of aim or intent

massasauga rattlesnake*- rattlesnake the north present in Michigan

Mida*- Native American name for a medicine man or sorcerer

mirthlessly*- without humor

morel mushrooms*- an edible fungi with a conical head and deeply pitted crevices

narcissism*- an excessive interest in or admiration of self, selfishness

Nawak'osis*- Native American name for marijuana

oblivion*- state of being forgotten

overwhelmed*- crushed, made helpless

ozone*- a blue gas discharged from lightning.

perchance*- by some chance

penchant*- a strong liking or taste for

periphery*- at the edge of one's vision

perusal*- a brief glance over

pippsissewa*- Native American name for wintergreen

psychopath*- antisocial personality prone to criminal and violent behavior

pungently*- sharp smelling

racking it up to*- to decide something

redolent*- sweet-smelling, fragrant

reverberated*- echoed

rife*- widespread, prevalent

ruminating*- chewing on

schizophrenic*- a person with a mental disorder characterized by hallucinations or delusions

stealthily*- secretly

succinctly- clearly and briefly

super-max*- federal prison for the most dangerous of criminals

switchbacks*- winding paths of gradual descent down a steep embankment

telepathically*- from mind to mind without speaking

toss my cookies*- throw-up, puke

traipse*- to walk or wander, trudge

trajectory*- path taken through the forest

trek- a long walk or journey

trepidation*- fear or alarm, dread

tyke*- a small child

unequivocally*- in a way that leaves no doubt

unwieldy*- not easily handled

usurp*- take illegally by force

verdant*- covered with green vegetation

wry*- twisted, distorted

The saga continues in Book 3 of

Conversations With Sasquatch

The Awakening

1

It is full blown winter on the ridge beside Big
Creek and the cedars and pines are dressed in cloaks
of the purest white snow. It is beautiful, though its
beauty is disguised in an undercurrent of deceit. The
muffled silence is but a trick up the sleeve of a polar
wind that is building to blow. For now, however, I
take solace in the fact that Big Creek is a wonderland
to behold.

It has now been over a month since Demarcus
terrorized Decker and sent him packing back to Bay
City. This is my first trek into the woods since then,
with hopes that Loquius and I might meet for a
wintery escapade out of Big Creek into Cross Over. I
have been suffering from a case of cabin fever and
my body needs a good stressing to awaken from its
winter complacency.

Despite the harsh cold I have worked up a light sweat trudging around in the woods with my snowshoes. My legs are screaming in pain and beginning to cramp from the unusual motions and exertions. It's no mystery to me that I shouldn't get all sweated up in the cold, so I pause and prop my 30-30 against a tree and take a breather. I am about a quarter of a mile from where I had met Loquius for the first time in the spring of 2020.

As I wait, I can feel The Stone Without Time growing warm in my pocket. It has been turning on and off for the past several days. I have caught glimpses of Rutheeus and some of the other Sasquatch elders rustling about in the stone's depths. To my dismay, however, Loquius has been totally absent from all these wavering visions and I am becoming concerned. Where is my friend?

I pull the stone out into the cold hoping he might be there for my benefit, but all I see is a swirling fog without any discernible shapes.

I feel torn, especially about the gun. I have never brought one into the Big Creek woods for fear it would cause mistrust. But with winter set in, I don't feel secure without it. There are just too many uncertainties and dangers to being alone in the woods in February. Even coyotes or wolves present a danger I would never consider in the summer.

With my body cooled down, I pick up the 30-30 and move toward the destination of our previous meeting site. I am very aware that I am the only motion and sound in the area. As has been the case many times before, the hairs on my arms and back begin to prickle from the looming presence of a Sasquatch.

2

In a flash I find myself face to face with Demarcus.

I flick the safety off on the 30-30 and it suddenly feels like a peashooter instead of a weapon.

I have no qualms about shooting if I have to, but I I've promised myself I will only do so in self-defense.

Demarcus is standing motionless about ten yards away.

Any aggressive move toward me and I am afraid the bullets will fly. I am very aware that I will have little time to land a fatal shot before his big strides could overtake me.

"Demarcus," I say. "I have no idea why you were exiled here, but I have no fight with you."

"Loquius with you." Demarcus manages to utter in a clipped and guttural way. At least that is what it sounds like he is saying, though I cannot tell if it is a statement or a question.

"Loquius my friend," I say with my hand over my heart.

Demarcus looks around, seemingly searching for any sign that Loquius might be about.

"Fire stick," he says and points a finger at my 30-30.

"Yes," I say to him.

He shakes his head very slowly as if contemplating the consequences of the gun. Then very slowly he reaches behind himself and lifts the remnants of Decker's bent rifle up for me to see.

"Yes. I saw you do that. I am aware of your strength and power. I will not shoot as long as you mean no harm."

Demarcus once again nods very slowly. I am watching closely for any tension in his legs that would signal the intent to pounce. I am not taking anything for granted, but I am not seeing any signs of such aggression.

"You help Chiha Tanka."

Again, I cannot tell if he is asking or stating.

"Yes, at the bequest of Rutheeus," I say to him.

Once again, Demarcus is dead still with his deep set eyes locked on mine.

"No hurt," he says. "Humans teach us how to speak." He raises a hand and points in the the direction of Dead Horse Sink.

"You hurt humans?" I ask.

"Not hurt," he says. "We make cross."

Demarcus makes a cross with his huge index fingers.

"You promised the humans you wouldn't hurt them?" I ask.

"Yes. We promised. We make cross."

"Thank you, Demarcus. Can we make cross?"

Demarcus once again raises his arms and makes a cross with his index fingers. I slowly set down my 30-30 and return the gesture.

Afterword

Thank you for taking the journey. If you have made it this far then you are a true believer. You have looked into The Stone Without Time and know the future holds a promise of greater things to come.

It is a Sasquatch saying that all barriers and all freedoms are self-created and/or self-imposed.

It is on a generous diet of courage and wisdom that all great civilizations come to be. It is through even greater courage and wisdom that they are maintained and expanded upon by discipline and certainty.

We are the true caretakers of our own souls and the soul of the world on which we live and depend. Heaven is not just a place you go. It is a place you create. The same can be said for Hell.

Best Wishes,
Loquius, Master at Arms for the Sasquatch Council of Elders

Michigan author and artist, Richard Rensberry, lives in Fairview, Michigan with fellow author and illustrator, Mary Rensberry. Together they founded QuickTurtle Books® and **BooksMakeBooms.com**. They are authors, illustrators and publishers of over thirty children's books and custom books for small businesses and worthwhile causes.

More QuickTurtle Books

Conversations With Sasquatch, The Encounter
Sasquatch, A Rhyme for Kids
The Bigfoot Parchments
If I Were A Lighthouse
Keepers of the Light
Big ships
Good Thoughts Gathered Together
Christmas Christmas Everyday
Grandma's Quilt
I Wish I Could
Fairview Berries
Float the River
Butterfly Stomach
The Quest We Share
Maple Tree Elves
A Boy and His Dreams
and many more

For copies of any of our books, please email us for more information at:

maryandrichard@quickturtlebooks.com

or visit our shopping cart at:

https://www.booksmakebooms.com

If you enjoyed this book, please visit it on Amazon and leave a review to help others with your precious words. It means a lot to Indie authors like me.

Made in the USA
Middletown, DE
09 May 2021

39345840R10060

Conversations With

Sasquatch

Book 2
Cross Over

Richard Rensberry

Copyright © 2021, Richard Rensberry

Illustrated by Mary Rensberry

Cover art by Michael Payton

All rights reserved.

No part of this publication may be reproduced, stored in a retrieval system or transmitted in any form or by any means electronic, mechanical, photo-copied, recorded or otherwise, without the prior written permission of the publisher and authors.

Published by: QuickTurtle Books LLC®

https://www.booksmakebooms.com

ISBN: 978-1-940736-70-9
Published in the United States of America